This edition published by Parragon Books Ltd in 2014

Parragon Books Ltd
Chartist House
15–17 Trim Street
Bath BA1 1HA, UK
www.parragon.com

Written by Barbara Jean Hicks
Illustrated by Brittney Lee

978-1-4723-7747-0

Printed in China

A Sister More Like Me

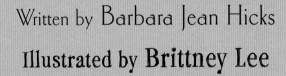

Written by Barbara Jean Hicks

Illustrated by **Brittney Lee**

Bath · New York · Cologne · Melbourne · Delhi
Hong Kong · Shenzhen · Singapore · Amsterdam

My name is
Princess Elsa.
I'm as royal as can be.

If the words look neat
and simple, then they
belong to me.

I'm her little sister,
Anna – I like colour,
noise and sunshine.

**When the words are bold
and crowded, you can tell
that they are mine.**

When you and I were little,
we were close as we could be.

I was happy you were Anna.
You were thrilled that I was me.

Till I had to hide my magic,
and our closeness
had to end.

I was still your older sister,
but I couldn't be your friend.

I followed you
around the house

and chattered like a bird.

I tried my best to please you,
but you never said a word.

That's when I started dreaming
about how my life would be ...
if I ever had a chance to have
a sister more like me.

I considered it my job to do
what needed to be done.
You were always and forever
finding ways to have more fun.

There were times you made me crazy,
though I tried to let you be,
as I wondered why I couldn't have
a sister more like me.

While I galloped on my pony
in the wind and rain and sun,
you were cooped up in the library –
and you thought that it was fun!

I'd have loved to have a playmate
who would join me up a tree.
I would have, if I could have had
a sister more like me.

And *I'd* have loved to have a friend who knew how to study,
I would have, if I could have had a sister more like *me.*

You needed peace
and quiet.

I was Princess Meet-and-Greet.

Your room was an explosion!

Mine was always clean and neat.

You were elegant and proper,
and you loved a fancy tea,

while I preferred a bright and
breezy picnic by the sea.

You didn't seem to care a bit about the way you dressed.
It was important, as a princess, that I looked my best.

You were the picture of perfection,
every day, no matter what.
I tried to understand you,
but the door was always shut.

Then one day I was
so dazzled when I saw
what you could be.
And I wondered …
did I *really* want a
sister more like me?

You showed me that you loved me,
and I suddenly felt free —
and truly glad I didn't have
a sister more like me.

You always did your duty,
and you always used your head.

You always listened to your heart
and followed where it led.

I'm very glad I *haven't* had a sister more like me.

With you around, without a doubt, I see things differently.

I was prickly as an urchin.

I was stubborn as a mule!
Now we try to work together –

it's our Sister Golden Rule.

You are bold and fearless, Sister,
and you have a loving heart.

You are poised and graceful, Sister,
and so wonderfully smart.

I'm so happy you are Anna and I'm pleased that I am me.

I'm thrilled that you are Elsa and I'm happy I am me!

But even more important — we are happy we are WE.

The End